GHOST DETECTORS

Don't Read This!

BOOK 6

BY
DOTTI ENDERLE

ILLUSTRATED BY
HOWARD MCWILLIAM

magic
Wagon

visit us at www.abdopublishing.com

A special thanks to Melissa Markham — DE
In memory of my own little white ghost dog, Mortimer—HM

Published by Magic Wagon, a division of the ABDO Group,
8000 West 78th Street, Edina, Minnesota 55439. Copyright
© 2010 by Abdo Consulting Group, Inc. International copyrights
reserved in all countries. All rights reserved. No part of this
book may be reproduced in any form without written permission
from the publisher.

Calico Chapter Books™ is a trademark and logo of Magic Wagon.

Printed in the United States.

Text by Dotti Enderle
Illustrations by Howard McWilliam
Edited by Stephanie Hedlund and Rochelle Baltzer
Cover and interior design by Jaime Martens

Library of Congress Cataloging-in-Publication Data

Enderle, Dotti, 1954-
   Don't read this! / by Dotti Enderle ; illustrated by Howard
McWilliam.
       p. cm. -- (Ghost Detectors ; bk. 6)
   Summary: When Malcolm gets a school assignment to write a
research report on a long-dead local hero who wrote a book
about his adventure-packed life, he is shocked to meet the
author's ghost, who reveals that he was a fake.
   ISBN 978-1-60270-695-8
   [1. Ghosts--Fiction. 2. Fraud--Fiction. 3. Schools--Fiction.] I.
McWilliam, Howard, 1977- ill. II. Title. III. Title: Do not read
this!
   PZ7.E69645Do 2009
   [Fic]--dc22
                                           2008055325

Contents

Take a Pick

Malcolm looked around the classroom at all the shocked faces. He waited for someone else to ask the question on all their minds. When no one did, he raised his hand. "You mean, we don't have a choice on who our report will be on?"

"Not this time," his teacher, Mrs. Goolsby, said. "I'm tired of reading endless research papers on movie stars and athletes. So this year, I've chosen the

subjects for the reports and you get to take a pick from them."

She held a paper bag filled with small strips of paper. On each strip was the name of a famous person. "Reach in and draw one out," she said, as she walked between the rows of desks.

Malcolm waited. He hoped to draw the name of a noted scientist or inventor. Most of the kids were groaning after reading their picks. Then his best friend, Dandy, reached in.

"Yes!" he cried, beaming with excitement. Malcolm couldn't wait to see who Dandy got.

Mrs. Goolsby finally made it around to Malcolm's desk. There were only a few strips of paper left. She shook the bag, then held it in front of him. He reached in and flicked one strip away.

Please be someone interesting! He held his breath as he drew a strip of paper out of the bag. He carefully unfolded it and read: Cooley Tucker. His heart sank. *Who was Cooley Tucker?*

Malcolm looked around the classroom. Most of the kids were jotting down the names they picked. Dandy was swaying in his seat, waving his strip of paper in the air. Clearly he was thrilled.

"Okay," Mrs. Goolsby said, once the last piece of paper had been selected. "This research paper is due a week from Friday. And I don't want you to just scour the Internet for information. Use the library, please!"

Malcolm waited until everyone was lining up for lunch before approaching Mrs. Goolsby. "Um . . ."

"Yes, Malcolm," she said, shuffling some papers on her desk.

"About my pick," he went on.

"Sorry," she said. "We can't change it. Maybe you can ask a classmate to trade with you."

"It's not that," he told her. "It's just that . . . I have no idea who Cooley Tucker is."

Mrs. Goolsby's eyes lit up. "Oh! You'll love researching him. He's a local hero."

"Really?" Malcolm asked.

"Oh yes. Using a telephoto lens of his own invention, he took the most spectacular pictures of Halley's Comet back in 1910."

Malcolm's dread was suddenly lifted. "That's so cool!"

"He made a fortune selling copies," she said. "You won't find much about him online, but his autobiography is in the public library. And there should be some newspaper articles from back then."

"Thanks so much!" Malcolm said. He grabbed his lunch and took his place in line. Cooley Tucker sounded like a real pioneer.

Malcolm couldn't wait to see the photos of Halley's Comet. He planned to visit the library right after school.

A Famous Pitcher

"So who'd you get?" Malcolm asked Dandy as they sat at the lunch table.

"I got a famous baseball player!" Dandy beamed. He dug into the Tuesday Lunch Special—chili pie.

Malcolm was confused. "Really? I thought Mrs. Goolsby didn't want any more research papers about jocks."

Dandy crunched on the corn chips. "It's not a jock. It's a girl baseball player. She

was a pitcher. She probably pitched for one of those lady leagues a long time ago."

"What?" Malcolm said. "Who is it?"

Dandy shifted the bite of chili and chips to the other side of his mouth, still munching. "Her name was Molly Pitcher."

"Dandy, " Malcolm hated disappointing his friend. "Molly Pitcher didn't pitch for a baseball team."

"Oh. Did she play softball?" Dandy shoveled more chili pie into his mouth.

"No," Malcolm told him. "She lived during the Revolutionary War. She got the nickname Molly Pitcher because she took a pitcher of water to the fighting soldiers."

Dandy stopped chewing. "She didn't play ball?"

"Not professionally," Malcolm said.

"Oh, geez," Dandy complained. "She never pitched a no-hitter?"

"I doubt it. But she was heroic."

Dandy stirred the bowl of mush in front of him. "Giving people water doesn't sound so heroic. Every time we eat at the Big Angus Steakhouse, the waitress fills my water glass. I don't think she's going to be getting any medals."

"It's heroic if the men were thirsty," Malcolm assured him.

"Maybe she had a fancy style of serving the water," Dandy said, perking up. "Maybe she could do magic tricks with it or something. I once saw a magician make water float up above a glass. That was really cool."

"Maybe she balanced the pitcher on her head," Malcolm added. "It could be an interesting report."

"Yeah," Dandy said, now stuffing more chili pie into his mouth. "I bet she could really handle that pitcher like a pro. So who did you get?" he asked Malcolm.

"I got Cooley Tucker."

Dandy froze, waiting. "Who's Cooley Tucker?"

"I didn't know either. He must have been an astronomer or something. According to Mrs. Goolsby, he's from around here and he took a bunch of awesome pictures of Halley's Comet."

"I've seen all kinds of pictures of Halley's Comet," Dandy said.

"Yeah, but the ones we've seen were taken in 1986. This Tucker guy took pictures of it in 1910."

"1910!" Dandy yelled, a little too loudly. "They had cameras in 1910?"

"Yeah," Malcolm informed him. photography was just catching on in those days. Not many people owned a camera."

Dandy's corn chips had now gone soft. He no longer crunched when he spoke. "You're lucky. You picked someone interesting."

"Well, so did you," Malcolm said. "You'll see. Want to go to the library with me after school?"

"Sure," Dandy answered. "I'll take lots of notes on this Molly Pitcher lady. Maybe I can find some really cool stuff about pouring water."

"Maybe," Malcolm told him. But Malcolm's mind was already on those photos and the amazing life of Cooley Tucker.

Shush!

Malcolm and Dandy raced up the front steps of the Franklin County Library. After pushing open the giant double doors, they headed for the bank of computers.

Dandy typed in *Molly Pitcher*. "Wow, there's a bunch of books on her! That's pretty good for someone who just poured water for folks."

"I think there's more to it than that,"

Malcolm said, looking up the information for his own paper.

"You think I'll need to read all of these books?" Dandy asked, scrolling down the computer screen.

"Just pick out a couple."

Malcolm only found one book on his subject. An autobiography called *Cooley Tucker: Genius At Work!*

Genius? That was a pretty bold title. He couldn't help but wonder, *if Cooley Tucker was such a genius, why was there only one book about him?* Then he remembered . . . the guy had written it himself.

Malcolm headed over to the shelves marked *Biographies*. It would be easy enough to find. Biographies were shelved by the last three initials of the person's last name.

He ran his fingers along the spine of each book . . . TRU . . . TSU . . . TUD . . . *Huh?* No TUC for Tucker. He double-checked. Rats! Maybe it was checked out. He hurried back to the computer. Nope. It clearly said: *Status: On Shelf.*

Malcolm went back and searched again. It just wasn't there. He had no choice. Malcolm went straight to the librarian, Mrs. Crutchmeyer.

His memories of Mrs. Crutchmeyer weren't very good. She continually shushed him when he wasn't making noise. She never let him check out more than eight books at a time. And the sound of her voice had made story time more like a trip to the dentist. Little kids even left crying.

Mrs. Crutchmeyer heaved herself forward as Malcolm approached. *"Shush!"*

Malcolm looked around. Yes, she was shushing him even though he hadn't spoken a word. He stood there a moment. Then he raised his hand.

She peered down her nose and through her cat-eye reading glasses at him.

"How can I help you?" she asked.

"I'm looking for the autobiography of Cooley Tucker," he said.

"Shush!"

Malcolm's jaw dropped. How could she shush him when he was only answering her question?

Mrs. Crutchmeyer sighed. "Is it misplaced again?" She heaved herself out of her seat and led Malcolm back to the biographies.

"It should be right here," Malcolm pointed out.

"Shush!"

Malcolm jumped again.

"We just can't seem to keep it here." Mrs. Crutchmeyer walked over to the section labeled *Fiction*. "No matter how

many times I reshelve it, it always winds up here." She pointed to the book tucked deep in the shelf between J. R. R. Tolkien and Jules Verne.

"Thanks," Malcolm told her.

"Shush!"

Malcolm flinched.

"Sorry," Mrs. Crutchmeyer said. "These darn allergies. And I left my tissues on my desk. *Shush! Shush!"*

"That's okay," Malcolm assured her with a sigh of relief now that he knew she wasn't shushing him on purpose. "I have what I need."

Mrs. Crutchmeyer hurried away and Malcolm looked for Dandy. He found him on the other side of the biography shelf, sprawled on the floor. He was leafing through a stack of books.

Dandy was flipping pages, three or four at a time. "I wonder which books I should check out."

"Which ones look the most helpful?" Malcolm asked.

Dandy scratched his head. "This one has a lot of cool illustrations."

"You don't want a picture book, Dandy."

"I'm going to check it out anyway. And these three." He held up three more books of varied lengths.

"Sounds good," Malcolm said.

They checked out the books and headed for the door. Malcolm waved toward Mrs. Crutchmeyer as they passed.

She waved back. *"Shush!"*

Beady Little Bird Eyes

O nce Malcolm got home, he dropped his backpack on the floor and headed to the kitchen. He was greeted with the combined smell of roasted potatoes and Grandma Eunice's foot ointment.

"Do you have to put that stuff on in here?" Malcolm's mom complained. "It's making my eyes water."

His great-grandma Eunice looked up. "I think I have a toenail fungus." She lifted her foot in air to show them.

Malcolm winced. Grandma Eunice's toenails were a glossy black. She squirted a large glob of ointment on her foot and rubbed hard.

"Every time I paint them they look like beady little bird eyes staring at me," she complained. "I hate being stared at by birds."

Just then, Malcolm's sister, Cocoa, stormed in wearing charcoal lip gloss, dark eyeshadow, and a licorice-colored dress. Malcolm thought she looked like an old black-and-white film. He wished it was a silent movie!

"Who's been using my Midnight Minx nail polish?" Cocoa demanded. She held out the bottle, shaking it. "What little bit that's left is dried to the bottom!" She glared at Malcolm.

He threw his hands up like he was dodging a punch. "Don't look at me. I don't use nail polish."

"Oh yeah? What about the time you took my Red Berry Delight?"

"Hey!" Malcolm exclaimed. "It was perfect for painting fake blood on my plastic vampire fangs."

"Mom!" Cocoa squealed.

"It was Halloween!" Malcolm added.

Mom didn't say a word. She just pointed to Grandma Eunice, who was massaging the ointment into her other foot.

Cocoa huffed. "Grandma! What are you doing?"

"Trying to get rid of these beady bird eyes," she said. "It's the worse fungus I've ever seen."

Cocoa stomped over to Grandma's wheelchair. "It's black nail polish." She held out the bottle for Grandma to inspect.

"Oh dear," Grandma said, looking it over. "Sorry, honey. Why don't you use my red polish?"

Cocoa rolled her eyes. "Because I don't want to look like I'm a hundred years old."

"Then why do you wear your hair like Albert Einstein?" Malcolm teased.

"Mom!"

Mom sighed. "We'll buy you some more nail polish later."

"Just don't buy her the kind that causes this fungus," Grandma said, rubbing her foot even harder.

"Aaaaaaaah!" Cocoa turned and thundered out of the kitchen.

Once things were quiet again, Malcolm asked his mother, "Have you ever heard of Cooley Tucker?"

Mom tilted her head. "Sounds familiar. Isn't he famous for inventing some kind of camera?"

"I think he invented a special telescopic lens," Malcolm said. "He took pictures of Halley's Comet with it in 1910."

"And they were some first-class pictures, too," Grandma Eunice said.

Mom and Malcolm both turned their attention to her. "You've heard of him?" Malcolm asked.

"Heard of him? My father bought some of his pictures back then. It was before I was born, but I remember seeing them when I was a little girl."

Malcolm tried to imagine Grandma Eunice as a little girl. "Do you know anything else about him?"

"We used to play by his old house on Morton Street," Grandma Eunice said. "The old coot always chased us out of his yard. Plumb loony by then."

Mom stood with her jaw hanging open. "Grandma, you remember all that?"

"Yeah, I remember him," she said defensively. Then, she paused and stared down at her black toes for a moment. "Or maybe it was Clark Gable I'm thinking of."

Malcolm grinned. He knew Grandma Eunice had forgotten she pretended to be crazy to get out of household chores. He played along to maintain their secret. "Maybe, Grandma," he said, as he rolled his eyes at Mom for added effect.

Malcolm headed down to his basement lab. He liked the peace and privacy he got there. Plus, down there he could turn on his Ecto-Handheld-Automatic-Heat-Sensitive-Laser-Enhanced Specter Detector. He'd bought it the summer before and had used it to hunt ghosts.

He'd even brought home a ghost dog, Spooky, and he used the specter detector to play with him.

Malcolm opened his backpack, ready to start reading up on Cooley Tucker. He pulled out his math book, his folders, his pencil case . . . he dug deeper. *Where was it?*

He turned his backpack inside out and shook it. *Where'd it go?* Malcolm remembered slipping the autobiography into his backpack just outside the library. It had to be here. He checked again. Nothing.

The autobiography of Cooley Tucker had mysteriously disappeared.

Back Again

After dinner, Malcolm backtracked to the library. Dandy came along to help.

Malcolm wondered if the book had slipped out of his backpack somehow on the way home.

"I would've heard it hit the sidewalk if it had fallen out," Dandy told Malcolm.

"Yeah, maybe," Malcolm said. "But you did have your nose in that Molly Pitcher

book.   And it was pretty noisy out."
Between the singing pizza guy at Pino's
Pizza Palace, and the jackhammer on Third
Street, it had not been a peaceful walk.

At the library, Malcolm grew nervous.
All he could think about was the huge
fine he'd have to pay if the book was lost.
He approached Mrs. Crutchmeyer's desk.

"Shush!"

"Hi," Malcolm said, not quite sure how
to ask.   "Uh, remember that book I
checked out?"

"Shush!"

He took that for a yes.   "I think I
might've left it here.   Did someone find it
and return it by any chance?"

Mrs. Crutchmeyer slumped a little.   She
stood up and led Malcolm back to the
fiction section.   Malcolm was relived to

see it was there, shelved out of place again.

"Oh good!" Malcolm cheered. "I thought I'd lost it."

"That always happens," Mrs. Crutchmeyer said with a sigh.

Before Malcolm could ask, Dandy piped up. "What always happens?"

"Shush!"

"I was just asking," Dandy said.

Mrs. Crutchmeyer drew a tissue from her pocket and blew her nose. "That book never stays checked out," she told them. "It somehow keeps returning on its own. And in the wrong section every time."

Malcolm scratched his head. "I don't understand."

Mrs. Crutchmeyer wiped her nose.

"Everyone who checks that book out leaves with it and then it goes missing. We don't know who's doing it, but someone takes it from them and puts it on this shelf."

"Is it someone who works here?" Dandy asked.

Mrs. Crutchmeyer shrugged. "I don't think so. It's been happening for years. I'm the only one who's worked here that long. It's like there's someone who doesn't want this book read."

"Well, thanks," Malcolm said, holding the book tight to his chest. "I'll do my best to hang on to it."

"Shush!" Mrs. Crutchmeyer sneezed. "Good luck," she added.

Malcolm and Dandy hurried away.

"I'm not letting this book out of my sight!" Malcolm said as they passed the pizza man. He wasn't distracted when the man twirled the dough high in the air while singing, "When the moon hits your eye like a big pizza pie . . . that's amore."

"That guy sure can sing," Dandy said.

"I'm not listening," Malcolm told Dandy. "No distractions."

When they turned onto Third Street the jackhammer shook the entire sidewalk. But Malcolm didn't even glance over.

When they arrived at Malcolm's house, they headed straight for the basement lab. Malcolm never took his eyes off the book as he sat down on the floor. Then he opened to the first page.

"Are you going to read that whole book tonight?" Dandy asked.

Malcolm looked at the table of contents. "I don't think so. It has 357 pages."

"Maybe they're mostly pictures of Halley's Comet," Dandy offered.

Malcolm flipped through. "Wow, look at these!" Right in the middle of the book were the glossy photos that Cooley Tucker had taken. They were like no other comet pictures Malcolm had seen.

The comet looked like a giant fireball coming right at him, the swooshing tail trailing behind. "These are awesome."

"Yeah," Dandy said. "That Cooley Tucker guy was some photographer."

"Now I'm curious. I'm going to read as much as I can tonight."

"Well, fill me in tomorrow," Dandy said, rising to leave.

Malcolm made it to page 96 when his eyes started to droop. Cooley Tucker was amazing, but even his exciting adventures couldn't drive the sleep away. Malcolm dozed off with his head resting on page 117. He slept like that for about an hour.

Whoa! he thought, jolting up. He looked at his watch. Oh no. It was way past his bedtime. Malcolm rubbed his drowsy eyes, then reached down for the book. But it was long gone.

Monkey in the Middle

Malcolm was now suspicious. He slid his specter detector into his backpack before heading off to school. The day dragged like a wet mop, but finally Malcolm was free to head back to the library. He had to know what was going on. Of course, Dandy kept him company on the way.

"Did you know that Molly Pitcher's name was not really Molly Pitcher?" Dandy asked as they hurried along.

"Yeah, I knew that," Malcolm said.

"Her real name was Mary," Dandy offered. "The name Molly Pitcher is like a nickname."

"Yeah," Malcolm repeated. He was listening, but not really.

"And she didn't just serve water like the waitress at the Big Angus Steakhouse. Her husband was a soldier, and when he got wounded, she took over the cannon."

"That's pretty awesome," Malcolm said.

Dandy's eyes lit up and his voice was excited. "There's even a story about a cannonball zooming right between her legs!"

Malcolm smiled at Dandy. "See? You did get a great subject for your report."

They rounded the corner and headed into the library. Mrs. Crutchmeyer's face

twisted up a little when she saw them.

"Shush!" She pointed toward the fiction section. "Just couldn't hang on to it, could you?" she said as they passed her desk.

"I managed to read nearly half of it before it disappeared," Malcolm told her.

"Shush! Well, that's more than most," she assured him.

Malcolm had to search a little harder for the book this time. It was back on the fiction shelf, but stuck behind some other books. Malcolm pulled it out.

"Let's see what happens," he whispered to Dandy. He unzipped his backpack and placed the book in, leaving it sticking up a bit. He set the backpack on the floor several aisles over, then pretended to be searching for another book.

"What are we doing?" Dandy asked. Before Malcolm answered, Dandy followed his example and grabbed a book off the shelf and thumbed through it.

Malcolm watched from the corner of his eye. "We're seeing if the book stays in my backpack."

They both waited and watched. Several people were careful to step around the backpack while browsing for books. One kid accidentally kicked it a little. But Malcolm still left it there on the floor.

"Do you think the book is going to magically jump back on the shelf?" Dandy whispered.

"I don't know," Malcolm said.

Several more minutes passed.

"I'm kinda getting hungry," Dandy said. "Can we go now?"

Malcolm wanted a snack, too. And he was getting tired of waiting. "I guess," he said. But just as he said it, his backpack fell over with a loud smack. Everything inside scattered onto the floor.

"Wow!" Dandy said, his eyes wide. "Did you see that? It fell over on its own."

Malcolm hurried over to scoop up his things. Papers, pens, textbooks, and even his specter detector had fallen out.

"Uh . . . where's the book?" Dandy asked.

"Not in the backpack," Malcolm assured him.

Cooley Tucker's autobiography was exactly where they figured—back on the fiction shelf.

"Holy smokes!" Dandy said. "I didn't even see it float in the air."

Malcolm pulled out his specter detector and switched it on. "Me either."

Two giggly girls were nearby. Malcolm waited until they were gone. Then, he switched the specter detector to Detect.

Immediately an old, thin ghost appeared on top of a reference shelf. He squealed like they'd caught him in the shower.

Malcolm reached for the book, never taking his eyes off the frail phantom.

The ghost flew down and snatched the book out of Malcolm's hand. "No!" he yelled. "Don't read this!"

"I knew it!" Malcolm exclaimed. "You're Cooley Tucker!" He snatched the book back.

The ghost made a grab for it again, but Malcolm tossed it to Dandy. When Tucker

charged toward Dandy, he threw it over the ghost's head to Malcolm.

"I don't think we're allowed to play Monkey in the Middle in the library," Dandy said.

The ghost reached toward Malcolm. Malcolm spun, then handed the book around to Dandy.

"You can't read my book!" the ghost cried.

Just one aisle over, Malcolm heard, *"Shush!"* He flipped off the specter detector and Cooley Tucker vanished.

"Did you find it?" Mrs. Crutchmeyer asked, rounding the corner.

"Yes, ma'am," Malcolm said. He tucked the book back into his backpack, and wasted no time heading home.

Why?

O nce he was back in his basement lab, Malcolm turned the specter detector back on.

Yip! Yip! Spooky bounced with glee.

"Hey, boy," Malcolm said, holding up his arm. Spooky loved hurdling back and forth over it. Sometimes he didn't quite make it over, but that was okay. He'd simply float through. Malcolm liked the way it tickled when Spooky went through him.

Dandy scanned the room. "Any more spirits here besides you, Spooky?" he asked.

Malcolm looked around. "I don't think Cooley Tucker followed us."

"But I bet he's the one who's been stealing the book and putting it back on the shelf," Dandy said.

Malcolm agreed. "Yeah, but when he shows up this time, I'll be ready." He pulled out his ghost zapper.

Dandy picked up an old tennis ball. "Fetch!" he told Spooky.

Yip! Yip! The ball rolled into the corner.

They watched Spooky try every way he could to clamp the ball in his mouth. "He just doesn't give up," Dandy said.

Malcolm settled back and opened Tucker's autobiography. "I just don't

understand. Why doesn't he want me to read it?"

"I don't think he wants anyone to read it," Dandy offered.

"But why?" Malcolm asked.

Dandy's lip twitched as he thought. "Maybe it has a typo."

"Lots of books have typing mistakes," Malcolm said. "That wouldn't be it."

"But what if it's a big mistake?" Dandy's lip twitched much faster. "What if they accidentally printed *she* instead of *he*? People might think he's a girl."

Malcolm held up his hand to stop Dandy from saying more. "Hang on. Cooley Tucker wrote this book himself. Why would he refer to himself as he? Wouldn't he write *I* or *me*?"

"Well, that's true," Dandy said, heading

over to retrieve the tennis ball that Spooky couldn't latch his teeth into.

Malcolm watched as Dandy reached through Spooky to get the ball. "There's got to be a better reason," he said.

Dandy shrugged. "Maybe it's the only copy and he's afraid if it's checked out, it'll get damaged."

Malcolm thought about that. "It is the only copy in the library. But I doubt it's the only existing copy." He hadn't thought to look online to see if there were any for sale.

"The thing is," Malcolm went on, "the guy was amazing. You wouldn't belive his life story."

"Really?" Dandy asked, pitching the ball across the room again. Spooky scrambled for it. *Yip! Yip!*

"Seriously," Malcolm said. "When he was a baby, his family abandoned him in the woods. He was taken in by a pack of wolves. He lived with the wolves until he was five years old."

Dandy's eyes grew large. "He was raised by wolves?"

"And that's not all. The man who found him hiding in the woods took him in and taught him how to talk. Until then, Cooley only growled."

"That was lucky," Dandy said.

"Only the man turned out to be some sort of pirate. Cooley sailed with him for eight years, robbing other ships and swindling people in different exotic ports."

Dandy was no longer paying attention to Spooky. "Then what happened?"

"I was up to the part where his pirate father was arrested. Then, Cooley was taken in by a wealthy politician who sent him off to boarding school."

"If my life were that exciting," Dandy said, "I'd want everyone to read about it."

Malcolm nodded. "I know. There's got to be something in there that he wants hidden. I'm going to try to read the rest tonight."

"Read real fast," Dandy said.

"I will." Malcolm held up the specter detector. "And I plan to leave this on so I can see if he sneaks in here to snatch the book back."

Nothing but the Truth

Malcolm read fast. His eyes got droopy and he yawned over and over. But, he finally made it through.

As he finished, he was already thinking about what to include in his research paper. He'd never read of anyone who'd lived such a full life and accomplished so much.

Wolves, pirates, hot air balloons, wildlife photography. Sadly the wildlife

photos had been destroyed in a fire, so Tucker couldn't include them in his book.

Malcolm slammed the book shut, yawned, then stretched. Spooky had been yipping and bouncing and chasing some fuzz when suddenly, *Grrrrrr* . . .

"What is it, boy?" Malcolm said. But he already knew. From a far corner, Cooley Tucker emerged. Malcolm grabbed the ghost zapper.

"Can I have my book now?" Tucker asked.

"No," Malcolm said. "I need it for my report."

"Couldn't you pick someone else? Galileo? George Washington? Mark Twain?"

"I didn't exactly get to pick," Malcolm informed him. "My teacher did." He

didn't think it was necessary to tell Tucker about choosing his name from Mrs. Goolsby's paper bag.

Tucker looked at the ghost zapper. "Are you going to use that thing on me?"

Malcolm turned to set it down. "I should, but I really want some answers."

Tucker sighed and sat down . . . on nothing. He just sort of floated there on an invisible chair. "I really don't want you to do your report on me."

"Why? You're the most fascinating person I've ever read about!"

"Really?" Tucker said. "More fascinating than Captain Ahab? Or King Arthur? Or Dr. Jekyll?"

"But those are made-up characters," Malcolm said.

"And so am I," Tucker told him.

Malcolm was more confused than ever. "That's impossible. You're a ghost. So you had to have been a living, breathing person before."

"Breathing, yes. Living, no."

"I don't get it," Malcolm said.

Tucker uncrossed his legs and leaned forward. "I was born in Madisonville, twenty miles from here. My parents were turkey farmers."

"You weren't raised by wolves?"

"I'd never even seen a wolf until I was an adult. And I was never taken in by a pirate or a wealthy politician. Although my uncle ran for town council in 1904."

"Did he win?"

Tucker 's face dropped. "No." Tucker sighed again then went on. "So you see what I'm saying? None of it's true. I'm a

fraud. That's why I keep moving the book to the fiction section."

"Why didn't you just hide it somewhere?" Malcolm asked.

"I've hidden four already," Tucker said. "That librarian just keeps ordering new ones."

Malcolm thought about what Tucker was saying. He didn't want to believe the truth. But more importantly, he didn't want his research paper to be a pack of lies.

Then he remembered. "Wait. What about these?" Malcolm opened the book to the pictures of Halley's Comet. "These are wonderful."

Cooley buried his face in his ghostly hands. "Let me tell you how I really took those photographs."

The Flight of Halley's Comet

The ghost walked over to Malcolm and peered down at the photographs in his book. Then he sat down—again in midair—and began.

"I hated turkey farming," he said. "Turkeys are big, dumb birds. They're messy. Feathers are everywhere. And people only really like them at Thanksgiving."

Malcolm thought about the turkey farm he'd visited on a third-grade field trip. There were lots of feathers!

"I had to get away," Cooley continued. "I worked hard and saved my money. What I wanted more than anything was to be a newspaper photographer. So when I saved enough money, I bought a brand-new Kodak Brownie camera. It was the latest model. I packed up everything I owned and came to the city."

Malcolm noticed the gloom in Tucker's voice. He knew this was going to be a sad story.

"I found a place to stay at a boarding house," Tucker went on. "And took a job at the Five and Dime."

"The Five and Dime?" Malcolm asked. "Sounds like a bank."

"No. A Five and Dime was just a small store. They sold a little of everything and most every item cost either a nickel or a dime."

"Oh," Malcolm said. "Sounds a lot like the dollar store."

Tucker shrugged. "I spent most of the day working at the Five and Dime, but in the afternoons I'd search out exciting things to photograph. I just needed one big break. One special photograph.

"I waited for some big news to break— a house fire, a trapped pet, a collapsing building. But I mostly just took pictures of flowers and friends and stray cats. My photos got better with practice, and I even built a darkroom in my closet so I could develop the film myself."

"Wow," Malcolm said. "I bet that was great."

"At the time," Tucker told him. "But I was still searching for my big break. Then in April 1910, I heard about Halley's Comet and how it would be visible in a couple of weeks.

"Some folks were a little scared, but most were excited. Especially me. I knew if I could take photographs of it, I'd surely get a spot in the local paper. So I ordered a new role of film and I waited.

"Lots of people headed up Old Baldy, the small mountain on the edge of town. You know which one I mean?" Tucker paused for Malcolm to answer.

"Yeah," Malcolm said. "They still call it Old Baldy."

"There was a big crowd there. And a couple of people had telescopes. I got to look through one. It was amazing!" Tucker's face actually lit up as he said it.

"So I took some pictures. A lot of people asked for copies and even paid me fifty cents each in advance. I made more money that night than I did working a whole week at the store."

"It sounds great," Malcolm said. "I bet you made a bundle afterward, too."

Tucker nodded. "But I should've given the money back."

"Why?" Malcolm asked.

"When I went to develop the pictures, too much light leaked into the darkroom. Instead of Halley's Comet, I got a picture of the night sky with this round glob of light smeared in the middle."

Malcolm looked at the photos again. "This isn't Halley's Comet?"

Tucker slumped. "It an overexposure. But it looked like a giant comet. I didn't

want to give the money back, so I made up a wild story about inventing a special lens. Everyone loved me. I was a hero.

"My legend grew. People admired me. They thought I was a genius. I didn't want them to know that I was really just a turkey farmer from Madisonville. So I wrote this autobiography."

Malcolm closed the book. "Wow," he said. It was all he could muster.

"So please don't do the report," Tucker begged. "It only makes me feel worse."

"But if I don't do this research paper, I'll fail."

"Please?" Tucker pleaded.

"Okay," Malcolm assured him. "I'll think of something."

And with that, Cooley Tucker took his book and left.

Prove It

"What did you just say?" Dandy asked the next morning before school. Malcolm had filled in Dandy about his visit from the ghost of Cooley Tucker. They strolled down the hall, heaving their heavy backpacks.

"I said, I have to tell Mrs. Goolsby that Tucker is a fraud," Malcolm answered.

Dandy picked some sleep gunk from his eye. "Maybe she'll assign you a different person to write about."

"I wish," Malcolm said. "But first, I have to convince her."

Dandy rolled the gunk into a teeny ball and flicked it away. "Just tell her the truth."

Malcolm laughed. "The truth? That I actually had a conversation with Cooley Tucker?"

Dandy shrugged, causing the straps on his backpack to slip down his arms. "It's not like she doesn't believe in ghosts."

"That's true," Malcolm agreed. He thought back to the beginning of the school year. Mr. Goolsby had haunted the school to let their teacher know he loved her. After Malcolm showed her the pictures, things had gotten much better. But they still had plenty of schoolwork to keep them busy!

Malcolm and Dandy settled into their desks, and Malcolm waited. *Should he tell Mrs. Goolsby now? Should he wait until after school?* No. Putting it off would just make things worse.

Malcolm approached Mrs. Goolsby's desk. Mrs. Goolsby looked up with a smile. "Good morning, Malcolm."

She was in a good mood. Great! Malcolm lowered his voice, not sure exactly how to say it. "Mrs. Goolsby," he started, "about my paper . . ."

"What about it?" she asked, her smile fading.

Uh-oh. "Well," he said, "it's just that the stuff in Mr. Tucker's autobiography—"

"Exciting, isn't it?" Mrs. Goolsby said. Her smile was back.

"Yes, but . . . ," he hesitated.

"But what, Malcolm?"

"None of it's true," Malcolm spat out. There, he'd said it.

Mrs. Goolsby's smile turned completely upside down. "And what are you basing this on?"

Should he tell her the whole truth? Would she understand? "Do you really believe he did all those things?"

"Why wouldn't I?" she asked. "What proof is there that he didn't do those things?"

"What proof is there that he did?" Malcolm countered.

"Photographs, for one," she said.

Malcolm waited, not sure what to say. He wanted to tell her about Tucker's ghost, but it just didn't seem like the right thing to do.

"Malcolm," she said, calmly. "Unless you can bring me proof, you need to get busy on that report. Understood?'"

Malcolm nodded. "Yes, ma'am."

When he got back to his desk, Dandy passed him a note that asked, *How'd it go?*

Malcolm didn't write back. He just looked over at Dandy and shook his head no.

Dandy passed him another note. *So now what?*

Malcolm wished he knew! But one thing was for sure. He had to get the book back from Cooley Tucker so he could do the report.

A Solution

"**N**o!" Tucker said, tugging at the book.

"I need it," Malcolm argued, pulling with all his might. Even with Dandy's help, Tucker wouldn't let go.

"Boy, he's one strong ghost," Dandy said, trying to pry the book away.

Malcolm agreed. It was like the book was glued to Tucker's hands. But just when Tucker was winning the tug-of-war—

"Shush!"

Malcolm let go when Mrs. Crutchmeyer strolled by. Tucker quickly slid through the shelves to hide, causing the book to drop on the floor.

Malcolm grinned at the librarian. "Thank you, Mrs. Crutchmeyer."

She gave him a confused look. *"Shush!"*

Malcolm snatched the book up off the floor, and he and Dandy raced off.

"You think he'll follow us?" Dandy asked as they sprinted down the sidewalk.

"I'm counting on it," Malcolm said.

Back at his house, Malcolm switched the specter detector back on and waited. For a while, the only ghost that haunted his basement lab was Spooky. *Yip! Yip!*

"Okay," Malcolm said to Dandy. "Help me get this paper written." He pulled up a blank document on his computer.

Dandy walked over and stared at the screen. "But won't that just make Cooley Tucker mad?"

"Yep," Malcolm answered. "So let him come stop me." Malcolm opened Tucker's book, looking around. Then he began to type.

Dandy watched over Malcolm's shoulder. "Wow, Tucker could make up some whoppers, huh?"

"Yeah," Malcolm agreed. "It's a shame he didn't write fiction novels." He continued to type out his report.

Both boys were so busy with the report, they didn't notice that Spooky was bouncing and barking a warning. *Yip!*

Yip! Yip! Yip! Then his barking stopped completely.

Malcolm looked up from the computer. Tucker was kneeling in the corner, petting Spooky. Really petting him! Not like

when Malcolm's hands brush right through. Spooky panted, loving every minute.

Dandy grabbed the book and held on. "It's okay, Malcolm," he said. "I won't let him take it."

"I don't care if he does," Malcolm said. "He can't take my report. It's right here, in the computer."

Tucker sighed. "If I can move a book, I can surely hit a delete key."

"How do you even know about computers?" Dandy asked.

Tucker picked up Spooky and rubbed his chin. "You forget, I live in a library."

"I have to turn in this report," Malcolm said.

"But you promised you wouldn't," Tucker reminded him.

Malcolm slumped. "I know. But it's a school assignment. I'll get an F if I don't. And I don't know how to convince my teacher that this stuff isn't true. I can't just tell her that you confessed."

Malcolm felt bad for Tucker, but it wasn't his fault the guy decided to create a big fat lie. He should've confessed back when there were people who would listen. Back when it could've been reported in a newspaper. Suddenly Malcolm had an idea. "Hey!" he said. "What if you publicly confess?"

"Show myself?" Tucker asked.

"No, confess in writing."

Tucker stopped scratching Spooky's chin and scratched his own. "I'm not sure I follow."

"Me either," Dandy added.

Malcolm turned his computer around so Tucker could see the screen. "I can create all kinds of things with this. Including a fake newspaper article. We could put an old date on it so Mrs. Goolsby thinks it was printed back then."

Tucker's face brightened. "Back when I was an old man."

"So," Tucker said, sounding happy. "You'll write a fake article saying it was all a sham?"

"No," Malcolm said. "You will."

"I can hit a delete key," Tucker offered, "but that's about it."

Malcolm turned the computer around and brought up a fresh screen. "You just tell me what to type."

Extra! Extra!

Malcolm turned in his research paper a day early. Included was a printout of a newspaper clipping dated January 11, 1954.

B2 NEWS January 11, 1954

COOLEY TUCKER CONFESSES!

Photographer Cooley Tucker, who became famous for his outstanding photographs of Halley's Comet, has now come clean. Having built his fortune on sales of the famous snapshots, Mr. Tucker admits that it was all a farce. The photographs in question are not images of the well-known comet, but an overexposure of light that leaked into his darkroom. Mr. Tucker also admits to making up the story of his life, told in his autobiography, Cooley Tucker: Genius At Work! Mr. Tucker regrets having deceived the public and deeply apologizes for his actions.

"Amazing!" Mrs. Goolsby said. "How did you find this?"

Malcolm shrugged. "It's a long story." He didn't answer her question directly because he didn't want to tell her a fib. And truthfully, it was a long story.

"Well, I'm just glad he did the noble thing and told the truth," she went on. "All this time I thought he was a hero."

"Confessing to something like this is pretty heroic," Malcolm said.

Mrs. Goolsby smiled. "I guess it is."

Malcolm and Dandy headed back to the library that afternoon.

"Look, it's still in the fiction section," Dandy said.

Malcolm powered up the specter detector.

"Do you think he's still hanging around?" Dandy asked.

"I'm still here," Tucker said as he hovered above one of the lower shelves.

Malcolm held up his report, showing Tucker the A he'd gotten. "It worked."

Tucker lowered himself to the floor. "That's wonderful. We all got what we wanted."

"Not me," Dandy said, pouting his lip. "I only made a B on my Molly Pitcher paper."

"So the book is going to stay on the fiction shelf?" Malcolm asked Tucker.

"Yes. It seems a copy of that article got dropped onto Mrs. Crutchmeyer's desk.

She doesn't bother trying to put it in the biography section anymore."

"Good," Malcolm said. "And you won't have to wrestle it away from other kids trying to do a report."

"Although playing Monkey in the Middle was pretty fun," Dandy added.

Tucker's face sagged. "No one would want to do a report on me now that they know the truth. I'm a nobody. I never accomplished a single thing in my life."

Malcolm smiled and pointed to the book. "Sure, you did. Not many people could write 357 pages of great stories. You should have been a writer, not a con man."

Tucker brightened at Malcolm's words. "You know," he said. "I still could be."

Malcolm waited, not sure what he meant.   Tucker waggled a ghostly eyebrow. "I write and you type?"

"Why not?" Malcolm said.   "But only on weekends."

Tucker extended his hand.   "It's a deal!"

Malcolm tried to shake, but his fingers went right through Tucker's palm. Malcolm laughed, thinking he could definitely write some pretty exciting stories of his own.

FIVE MORE WAYS TO DETECT A GHOST, SPIRIT, OR POLTERGEIST

26. A spirit may move an item it thinks it owns! Keep track of things that move on their own—they are definite signs of ghosts.

27. Bring your Ecto-Handheld-Automatic-Heat-Sensitive-Laser-Enhanced Specter Detector with you everywhere.

28. Your ghost pets can detect other poltergeists. Watch them for suspicious activity.

29. Listen to the stories told by older people, including grandparents and neighbors. Remember, Mrs. Crutchmeyer always said the library was haunted, but no one believed her.

30. Always believe in ghosts. If you don't believe, you will never see them. All they really want is someone to talk to!